Note to Parents

Reading books together can be one of the most pleasurable activities you share with your child. Young children love to spend time with their parents, and the opportunity to be the focus of your undivided attention. To get the most out of reading together, try to find a relaxed time that suits your family. Remember, reading should be fun, so show your enthusiasm and this will transfer to your child. If he or she is wriggling away, leave it for another occasion.

First Time Stories show familiar situations from everyday life that young children can relate to easily. Repetition helps children understand, so I suggest you read this book together more than once. You can use the story as a chance to talk about similar situations in your own child's life. As you read, follow the words with your finger to show the connection of the written word to what you are saying. Encourage your child's imagination if he or she wants to tell a different story from the pictures. Above all, enjoy reading together!

Eileen Hayes
Parenting Consultant to the NSPCC

374145

FIRST TIME STORIES

Our New Baby

Heather Maisner

ILLUSTRATED BY Kristina Stephenson

KINGFISHER

Ben was running past the toyshop
when he saw a red tractor in the window.
He was so excited that he tripped and fell,
banging his forehead.

Later, a bump swelled up.

"There's a baby in here," he told Amy, pointing to the bump.

"Don't be daft," she said. "Babies only grow in mummies' tummies."

Mum's tummy had grown big and round. When Amy held her hand against it, she could feel the baby kick.

"I hope it's a girl," she said. "We can collect jewellery together."

"I hope it's a boy," said Ben. "We can play tractors and football together." He kicked a ball across the lawn and Figaro chased after it, crashing through the flowerbeds.

Mum and Dad cleared out
the spare room and began
making it ready for the baby.

"Paint it purple," said Amy.
Purple was her favourite colour.

"No, red," said Ben,
thinking of the tractor
in the toyshop.

But Dad chose yellow.
"Yellow's a good colour for a
boy or a girl," he explained.

Everyone agreed, even
Figaro, who knocked over
the paint pot, leaving a trail of
yellow paw prints across the floor.

Dad scrubbed Ben's old pushchair. Ben sat in it and Dad whirled him round the garden. He liked being pushed in a pushchair.

Mum sorted through a bag of baby clothes.

"Was I really as little as this?" asked Amy, holding up a tiny white cardigan.

Mum's tummy grew bigger and bigger. Sometimes she rested in the afternoon and Ben had to play babies with Amy.

"You must keep the house tidy for baby,"
Amy told him bossily, handing him a duster.
Then she cradled a teddy in her arms.

"Hush now, baby is falling asleep," she
said, and Ben, Figaro and all the teddies
had to pretend they were falling asleep.

Mum packed a suitcase
ready to take to the hospital.

Ben packed a suitcase too, and hid it under the bed.

One morning, when Dad was
at work and Amy was at school,
Mum leant against the kitchen
table, clutching her tummy.

"I think the baby's ready,"
she said. She picked up the
telephone and began to dial.

Soon Gran arrived and Dad hurried home from work. He walked Mum out to the car, then ran back into the house to collect the suitcase.

"Wait for me!" said Ben.

But Gran lifted him up and cuddled him.

"You're staying here with me," she said. Ben watched from the window as Dad drove off with Mum.

Ben went with Gran to collect Amy from school.
Amy told her friends, "My mum's gone into hospital
to have the baby." She felt grown up
and important.

On the way home, they
passed the toyshop and
the red tractor had gone.
Ben was heartbroken.

Everything's changing,
he thought. *Nothing will
ever be the same.*

The next day, Amy and Ben went to the hospital to see Mum. She sat up against the pillows and hugged them close. Beside her bed stood a little cot.

"You've got a baby sister," she said.

"Great!" said Amy. "I always wanted a sister."

Ben bit his lip. He wanted to cry.

"The baby has a present for you," Dad said, handing them each a parcel. Amy pulled the wrapping paper from hers and opened the box. Inside was a silver necklace.

"I knew she'd love jewellery!"
she exclaimed.

Ben pulled off the wrapping paper and opened his box. "How did she know I wanted this?" he gasped, lifting out the red tractor that he'd seen in the toyshop.

"You can choose the baby's name," Mum told Ben, "as you didn't get a baby brother. Dad and I have made a list." Dad read out names from the list while Ben stared at the baby. Suddenly she wrinkled her nose, opened her eyes and blinked, just as Dad read out the name Tessa.

"Tessa," said Ben. "That's her name." Then she
began to cry. Ben bent forwards and whispered,
"Don't cry, Tessa, you can play with the tractor too."

The publisher thanks Eileen Hayes, Parenting Advisor to the NSPCC,
for her kind assistance in the development of this book.

For Saul, Dominic and Alice – H.M.
For Hilary and Gordon – K.S.

KINGFISHER
An imprint of Kingfisher Publications Plc
New Penderel House, 283-288 High Holborn
London WC1V 7HZ
www.kingfisherpub.com

First published by Kingfisher 2004
2 4 6 8 10 9 7 5 3 1

A CIP catalogue record for this book
is available from the British Library.

ISBN 0 7534 0996 8

Printed in Singapore
1TR/0704/TWP/PICA(PICA)/150MA